Dark Cloud Strong Breeze

story by SUSAN PATRON
pictures by PETER CATALANOTTO

Orchard Books New York

Thanks to Pat, the beautiful Light in Ohio, and especially Chelsea — P.C.

Orchard Books, 95 Madison Avenue, New York, NY 10016

Manufactured in the United States of America. Printed by Barton Press, Inc.
Bound by Horowitz/Rae. Book design by Mina Greenstein.
The text of this book is set in 21 point Veljovic Medium. The illustrations are watercolor paintings reproduced in full color. 10 9 8 7 6 5 4 3 2 1

Library of Congress Cataloging-in-Publication Data
Patron, Susan. Dark cloud strong breeze/story by Susan Patron; pictures by Peter Catalanotto. p. cm.
"A Richard Jackson Book" — Half t.p. Summary: A cumulative rhyme relates the sequence of events that takes place before Daddy can get into the car where he has locked his keys.
ISBN 0-531-06815-3. ISBN 0-531-08665-8 (lib. bdg.)
[1. Automobiles — Fiction. 2. Locks and keys — Fiction. 3. Fathers — Fiction. 4. Stories in rhyme.]
I. Catalanotto, Peter. ill. II. Title. PZ8.3.P27355Dar 1994 [E] — dc20 93-4873

For my resourceful nephews,
Edward Tuttle and Benjamin Chun

—S.P.

To Michelle and Mariko—
beautiful nieces, wonderful artists

—P.C.

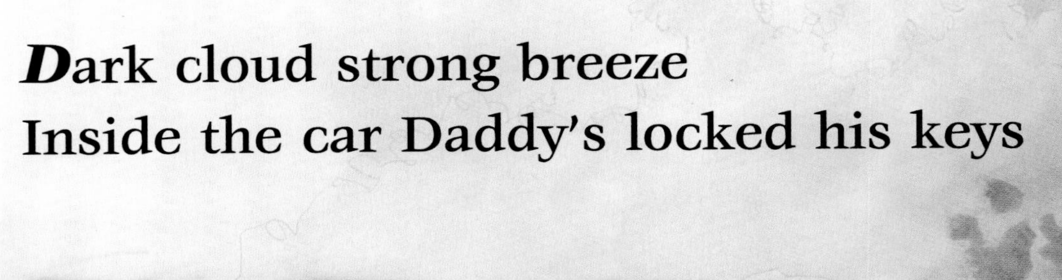

Dark cloud strong breeze
Inside the car Daddy's locked his keys

"Wait," I say to Daddy, jangle-me jore
"I can figure out how to open that door."

Dark cloud brisk breeze
"Hey, Mister Locksmith, will you help us, please?"

"Yes," says Locksmith, clicka-me clong
"If you get me a guard, both brave and strong."

Low cloud cold breeze
"Hey, good Dog, will you help us, please?"

"Yes," says Dogger, thumpa-me thorm
"In exchange for a shelter, dry and warm."

Gray cloud strong breeze
“Hey, Mister Grocer, will you help us, please?”

"Yes," says Grocer, smasha-me smit
"If you get me a mouser, lickety-split."

Rain cloud damp breeze
"Hey, Mrs. Cat, will you help us, please?"

"Yes," says Catty, swisha-me swhy
"If you show me a being more lovely than I."

Storm cloud wet breeze
"Hey, small dancer, will you help us, please?"

"Sure," says Butterfly, flutter-me flance
"I'll be happy to help you by dancing a dance."

Then rain begins falling, pitter-me pat
And wind gets stronger, whoosha-me that

SMITH
COMPANY

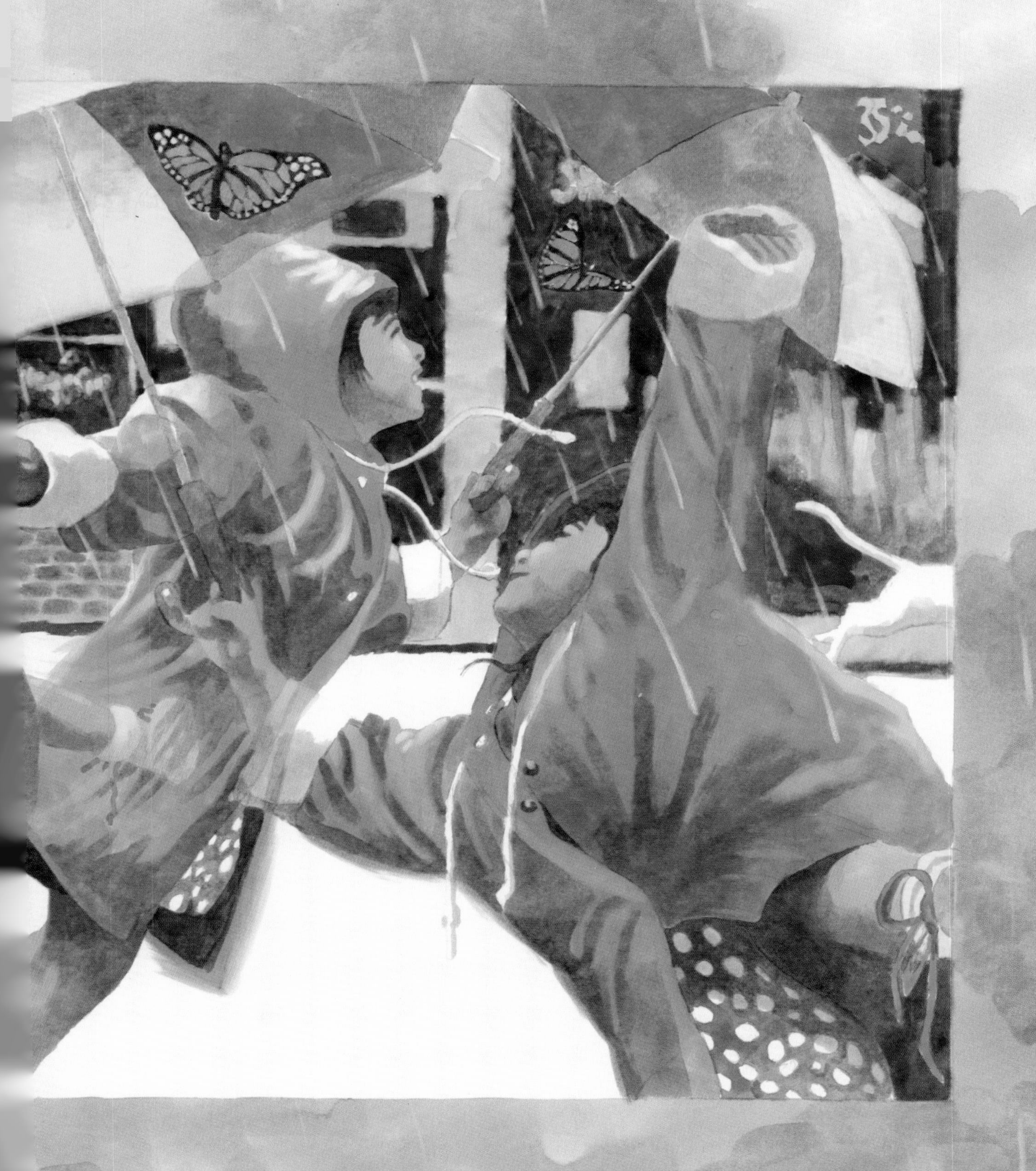

Butterfly dances, flutter-me flance
Butterfly flutters, happy to dance

CLEANERS
PAIN
WALLCOVE

Cat scares mice away, smasha-me smit
Cat scares mice away, lickety-split

CLEANERS

A shelter of boxes, thumpa-me thorm
A shelter of boxes, dry and warm

CLEANERS
PAINT &
WALLCOVERING

Dog guards the lock shop, clicka-me clong
Dog guards the lock shop, brave and strong

The car gets unlocked, jangle-me jome
The car gets unlocked, and we drive home

CLEANERS
PAINT &
WALLCOVERING

KET
MITH
COMPANY

Dark cloud strong breeze
Oops! Daddy's looking for his other keys

Well, I'm thinking, jangle-me jine
Daddy's lost his house key, but I have mine!

95-78

E
P

Patron, Susan.

Dark cloud strong breeze.